Once upon a time in China, every village had its own tax collector. The tax collectors would go to each house, and collect the taxes owed to the emperor. Then they would send it all to the palace. However, in one village the tax collector was not an honest man!

This tax collector would go around and collect the taxes, but then he would only send some of them to the palace. He kept the rest for himself. Sometimes a person did not have all the tax they owed. Then the tax collector would threaten to lock them up unless they gave him other things, such as animals or vegetables, or even their houses.

The villagers did not like or respect this tax collector. They would avoid him whenever they could. If they saw him heading their way, they would try to hide or pretend they were not at home.

One day, a boy was talking to his friend who lived in the next village. They decided that they would play a trick on the tax collector to show how dishonest he was. The boys dug up a small pear tree and put it into a pot.

In the morning, the boy's friend carried the pear tree in its pot to the next village and into the market square. The tax collector was waiting, looking for strangers that he could trick and take taxes from. He spotted the boy and walked over to where he had put down the pear tree.

"You have to pay the emperor a tax to bring that pear tree here and sell it," said the tax collector.

The boy looked sad. "But until I have sold this magic pear tree, I haven't got anything to give you," he replied.

"A magic pear tree you say?" said the tax collector.

“What is magic about it?” The tax collector wanted to know.

“Well,” said the boy, “It is a very rare pear tree. If you pick one of the leaves and stick it to your forehead, you become invisible. Then you can do whatever you want.”

The tax collector quickly claimed the tree for the emperor and hurried home.

The tax collector was very excited about the magic tree, which of course he was going to keep for himself. Once he got home, he picked a leaf and stuck it to his forehead. Then he went back out to the market square to see if it really was magic.

There were lots of villagers about as it was a market day, but they all ignored the tax collector and pretended they couldn't see him in case he took more taxes from them. He walked up to the baker's stall and took a bun. The baker pretended not to notice.

"It really is a magic tree!" exclaimed the tax collector.

Next, he took an apple and some vegetables from the grocer's stall. Next, he took a hat (because his hat was a bit old and this one would make him look even more important). All of the stall holders looked away and pretended they could not see him.

"It really is magic," he whispered joyfully. "I can do anything I wish and no one will see me!"

Just then, there was a lot of noise and a huge golden carriage arrived in the village. Everyone looked to see who it was.

“It’s the emperor’s carriage!” everyone exclaimed. “Look at all the gold and jewels, and the guards.”

On the back of the carriage hung a golden birdcage with a fantastic exotic bird in it. The emperor had just been given the bird in another village that he had visited that morning.

The greedy tax collector looked at the bird and the golden cage.

He rubbed his hands together and mumbled, “I'll be rich if I have that, and I'll never have to collect taxes again.”

Then because he was invisible and could do anything, he walked straight up to the emperor's carriage and unhooked the cage.

The guards looked at him in amazement.

"How dare you steal from the emperor," the head guard shouted. "Arrest him now!"

The guards rushed over. The tax collector saw that he had been tricked and started crying.

"I was tricked," he cried. "The boy told me that I would be invisible."

The emperor and the guards listened to the tax collector.

“You should not have tried to steal anything anyway, and certainly not from the emperor,” said the head guard. “You are under arrest and will be going to jail.”

All of the villagers came to see the greedy tax collector being taken away.

The boy and his friend were sitting in a corner of the square, looking on and smiling.

"Well," said the first boy, "It just shows you shouldn't trust everything you are told by someone else."

"Indeed," said his friend nodding, "and now the tax collector really will be invisible, at least in this village!"